DR. TW

originated by Roger Hargreaves

Written and illustrated by Adam Hargreaves

The Doctor leapt out of the TARDIS and ran as fast as he could to keep up with Missy.

She had led him back in time to ancient Egypt.

"You're getting old and slow!" Missy laughed.

The Doctor frowned.

Old indeed.

He was a Time Lord.

He had lived for centuries.

Of course he was old!

But so was Missy.

Because she was also a Time Lord.

The Doctor arrived inside the pyramid just in time to see Missy steal a sceptre from a sarcophagus.

"What is she up to?" muttered the Doctor.

Up to no good, came the reply in the Doctor's head.

But that was an easy answer.

Nowadays, it seemed like there was no good in Missy.

She acted all bad, but the Doctor knew better.

Just like the Doctor, Missy could travel through time.

But she used a vortex manipulator on her wrist.

The Doctor followed.

Back in time.

Back in time to the Tower of London.

Now Missy was stealing the Crown Jewels.

"Stop!" cried the Doctor.

But it was too late.

"Just for once I wish I could arrive early," huffed the Doctor in frustration.

He followed her again through time to Japan.

Where Missy had stolen a gold statue.

"Too slow!" cried Missy.

And then she was gone.

"I think I'll call you Doctor Slow," called out Missy when the Doctor caught up with her in Russia.

Now she had stolen a jewelled egg.

The Doctor was puzzled.

Why was Missy stealing all these jewels?

Were they Christmas presents?

Was she going to open a jewellery shop?

Was she going to sell them and buy a yacht and sail round the world?

All of these thoughts seemed very unlikely to the Doctor.

Missy loved to cause trouble.

The sort of trouble that might destroy the Earth!

Of course, thought the Doctor, *that is exactly what she's trying to do.*

The Doctor was not at all happy.

He had just realized something else.

All this chasing Missy through time meant he had missed lunch.

And now he was hungry.

But he had to keep going.

Their next destination back in time was the Wild West.

Missy had stolen a bag of gold dust.

And then the Doctor was in Paris.

But he had forgotten to leave the horse in the Wild West.

It was chaos.

And, in the chaos, Missy stole a diamond ring.

Finally, the Doctor caught up with Missy a very long way back in time.

In the Stone Age.

And finally the Doctor was there in time.

"You think I'm too slow to work out what you are doing, don't you?" said the Doctor. "But I'm quicker than you think."

The Doctor then emptied a bag of Cybermats on the ground.

"You thought you could fool me by taking all those jewels?" he added. "I retraced our chase and found these Cybermats left behind in each spot."

"Well, clever old you. Do you know what my plan was?" asked Missy.

"Haven't a clue," said the Doctor. "All I know is that I have saved the world."

"But you have to allow me to explain my devious plan!" whined Missy.

"No, don't care. I'm off now!"

"Where are you going?" asked Missy miserably.

"Back in time," replied the Doctor. "Back in time for something far more important."

"But what could be more important than hearing all about my dastardly crime?" cried Missy.

"Lunch!"